A LIFE OF TEARS

By: Barbara Smith

Order this book online at www.trafford.com
or email orders@trafford.com

Most Trafford titles are also available at major online book retailers.

Printed in Victoria, BC, Canada.

ISBN: 978-1-4269-2820-8 (sc)

*Our mission is to efficiently provide the world's finest, most comprehensive
book publishing service, enabling every author to experience success.
To find out how to publish your book, your way, and have it available
worldwide, visit us online at www.trafford.com*

Trafford rev. 03/17/2010

 www.trafford.com

North America & international
toll-free: 1 888 232 4444 (USA & Canada)
phone: 250 383 6864 ♦ fax: 812 355 4082

*Dedicated to my mother, the kindest person
I've ever known.*

Chapter One

Summer of 1912 -
A coal camp somewhere in West Virginia

I refuse to cry. I won't cry any more. I have had my time with that and it didn't do any good. They are still going to make me do it.

As I walked down the rugged path to the company store, I relived the last few hours at home. When I awoke this morning, I never dreamed the day would bring the misery to me that it has. I got up early and started the fire for Mama. She's pregnant again. What number is this? I can't even remember.

I'm the oldest girl. Twelve years old. The only ones older are boys, John and Sam. I love my family. I will work till I drop but they still are going to make me marry that man who is Papa's friend. They say it will ease their burden on the household expenses and care of the other kids. I had to quit school last year and I didn't complain because I want to help my family but this will take me away from them. I don't know anything about being a

1

wife. What will it mean? I will have to move in with this man and may be do things with him I don't want to do or won't like. Please, God. Don't let them punish me like this.

Arriving at the store, I walked in to purchase the lard Mama needed. There next to the old wood stove stood my nightmare. He's tall and slim and has a shock of wavy red hair. Those blue eyes are looking at me as if he already owns me.

"Mr. Cooper, please may I have a pound of lard and put it on my daddy's bill."

"Sure, Rosie. How's the family? Your Mama and the rest of the kids."

"Every one's fine, Mr. Cooper. Mama needed this for our supper. Thank you."

As Mr. Cooper handed me the wrapped can of lard, I felt like running out the store but I can't let my nightmare know I am afraid of him. Walk slowly, Rosie. Don't rush. But once I was out the door, I ran up the path as quickly as I could, panting for breath.

"Mama, I'm home with the lard. Mr. Cooper put it on our bill."

"That's fine, Rosie. Thank you, Honey."

"Mama, can we talk about what you told me this morning?"

"No, Rosie, we can't. It's already been decided. Willie told your Daddy he would take good care of you and it will help us out a lot. Your Daddy works so hard in the mines and that will take one load off him. It's not like Willie is old. He's only 19 and has a good job so I don't know why you are so against this."

"Because, Mama, I don't want to leave you and the others. I'll work even harder if you will only change your mind. You will need me when this baby comes".

"No, Rosie. You have to go and your sister, Leila, will take your place. She will be leaving school as soon as you are gone and soon another one of your brothers will be going into the mines, so the load will be lighter on your Daddy.

"But, Mama - you know Leila isn't strong. She can't do the work I can. She'll get sick again."

"She'll have to do it. We all have to carry our load and trials in the family. Whatever they may be."

"But, Mama. I don't know anything about being a wife."

"You don't have to know, Rosie. You're not suppose to know. Willie will know and he will teach you. That's the way life is. He will be your husband and you will do what he says. The main thing is to make his life comfortable. He will let you know what he wants."

I turned away then, knowing nothing else I could say would move her. I have to get outside and get some air. I think I am going to be sick. How can I leave my brothers and sisters and live with a man I don't even know. I don't know how this situation came about except this Willie man worked with my daddy in the mines and when I would go the store or play with my brothers and sisters, I could see him watching me. It gave me an odd feeling but I had no idea that he wanted to wed with me. I don't think I ever even said hello to him.

Once outside, I flew up the mountain where John, my favorite brother, and I use to play. Maybe I could make some kind of sense of this if I would just sit and think calmly about what was happening to turn my life around.

I didn't want to cry any more but in spite of it all, I began to sob. I cried so hard I was shaking and simply couldn't stop. I couldn't calm down enough to think. If I had some place to go, I would run away. But I didn't have any place to go.

Then, almost as if I imagined him, there he stood. Right in front of me. He had seen me fly out the door and had followed me to my secret place.

"Why are you crying, Rosie? I don't want to make you unhappy or sad. I want to marry you and live a good life with you. I have been watching you for the past 6 months and you have grown up so much lately that I have come to care a great deal for you. In fact, I love you."

"I don't know anything about love, Mr. Harrel. I'm only twelve years old. I don't want to leave my family. I don't know anything about you."

"I know you're young, Rosie, but it's time for me to marry and you're the one I want to do it with. I have a good job in the mines, we'll have our own home, at least it's ours and the mining company's, and I will always be good to you."

"I guess I have to do it but I'm scared. It's not like I don't like you. I don't know you and I'm just plain scared."

"I know. And I will always remember to take good care that I have a precious gift in you. Please trust me, Rosie. You won't regret it."

Chapter Two

Thereafter, it seemed Mr. Harrell was at our house every evening. He came in time for supper and stayed until we were ready for bed. He would come early and he and Papa would talk and then after supper, he and I would sit on the stoop (a porch on a company house was unheard of) outside and he would talk about things that I had no idea about . He was well-read and talked about things that I had never heard of. I had to leave school so early I knew very little about things. He made everything sound so interesting that I wish I could talk to him instead of just listen. I didn't know it but he was actually courting me and trying to let me get to know him - to take away my scared feelings about him.

After a few weeks, he would hold my hand while he talked. This was almost embarrassing as I had never been close to a man other than my Papa and brothers before. He seemed to be a gentle man and after a while, I began to feel at ease with him.

Almost before I could gather my senses and feelings together, we were married. The preacher only came around once a month, so we had to do it on his circuit trip or wait another month and Willie didn't want to wait. So there we were - in front of the preacher in my Daddy's house with our family standing by and us saying I do. I had on my best dress (which wasn't all that good) and the only pair of shoes I owned. Willie had to stoop quit a bit to brush my lips after the ceremony. He is so tall. Over six feet. I'm not quite five feet. We're almost strange looking side by side. But we'll have to get on with each other.

That little kiss was my first. What did I feel? Nothing. I haven't had anyone tell me what to expect. I am married to a stranger and I feel so weird. I was embarrassed to have him kiss me in front of all my family and his. My brother, John, had a fierce look on his face. He didn't like it either.

Mama fixed us a nice meal and even the preacher stayed to eat. Then as everyone began to gather their coats to leave, Mama said to me, "Rosie, be a good girl, now and mind your husband. He'll take care of you from now on."

How could I agree to mind my husband when I didn't know what to expect. What did he want with me? I'm just a kid. What do I have to do with him? Oh, God. Just let me die.

* * * * *

We left Mama and Daddy's house and I began to drag my feet. Maybe I could drop dead or maybe the ground would open up and swallow me. Then he would be sorry. So would my folks. They would be sorry they made me wed with this stranger.

"Come on, Rosie, it's not far. We can walk there in just a few minutes. I believe you will like what we have to begin our new life."

Willie had a little trouble finding the lamp to light so I waited at the door. When he found the light, I could see the house was just like the one I had left only not so many people. I finally remembered. Mama had had seven kids that lived. So now she has six. Until this one comes now and probably, she'll have more.

I walked around the house. It was clean with an almost new linoleum on he floor. The coal lamps had plenty of fuel in them. I guess Willie had filled them earlier and everything was neat and in it's place. The kitchen had the usual coal stove and table and chairs for two. There was a water basin with a pump for drawing water. There were no extras but I'm not use to that so it didn't matter. Willie had brought my clothes over (what few I had) earlier in the day. They would be hanging in the wardrobe along side of his. I feel so strange. Like a visitor here. What am I doing here with a man I hardly know.

"Come here, Rosie. I want to show you the rest of the house. The toilet is out back but we have two bedrooms. Ours and one I hope for our first baby."

"Baby! Oh, God. What are you saying?"

"Calm down, Rosie. Not right now but soon, I hope. Get undressed and let's get in bed. It's getting late."

I went to the bureau to look for my intimate clothes and pulled out an old homemade nightgown. Thank goodness it would cover me up completely. As I started to undress, I turned my back to him and began with the buttons on my best old dress. "Are you going to watch me undress?"

"Well, I won't if you don't want me to but I'd like to. You're my wife now and we belong to each other just like the bible says."

I continued to undress with my back to him and pulled my gown over my head before I completely took off my undergarments. I folded my clothes and placed them on a stool on the far side of the room. I walked around the bed and got in on the other side with him still sitting on his side fully clothed. When he stood up to remove his shirt and undershirt, I pulled the cover up as far as I could under my chin. Then the shirt came off and I have never seen so much skin. I had never seen a shirtless man before. Wide shoulders and blonde-red curling hair on his chest. Of course, I had never seen a nude man before. Then, he began to lower his pants and then his underpants and what I saw almost made me scream. I covered my head completely and started to moan in fear. What in the world was he going to do with what I saw protruding out from his lower body surrounded by a thatch of red hair.

I could feel the bed sink as he lowered himself in beside me and he sort of chuckled as he began to pull the sheet from my face. When he saw me, he then laughed out loud and said "Come here, Rosie. I am not going to hurt you. I told you I would always take care of you. I love you." Then he began to kiss me and nuzzle my neck all the while caressing my body, gradually lifting my gown up as his hand moved over me. He kissed me deeply and I began to relax when suddenly he stuck his tongue in my mouth. I stiffened up again but as he continued, I began to like it. What is this, I thought. But it doesn't feel bad. It feels - I don't know - Good isn't the right word. I had never had this feeling before. It made me feel in suspense of something going to happen. I could never explain this feeling.

Oh, God. What is happening to me? I never felt this way before. Then Willie put his big hand on my breast and began to knead it and tweak my nipple. Suddenly, he leaned down and took the nipple in his mouth and began to suck on it. I didn't know this happened with married people. Why would he want to suck on my nipple. That was for babies. I had watched Mama do it. I wish someone had told me what to expect. Then, I began to feel warm down in the lower part of my stomach. I wanted to move my body but I don't want him to think I liked what he was doing. The only thing I had ever heard was that a woman was to surrender (whatever that meant) to her husband and endure. I don't know what is happening to me. Surely there is something wrong with me. I don't think I should be feeling like this. I should hold myself stiff and not surrender to these wanton feelings.

When he raised his head, he smiled down at me and said, "This will be a good marriage. I can make you feel good and loved. You have already made me feel good by marrying me."

Then he shifted himself until he was on top of me. "Open your legs for me, Rosie. Let me in."

I was almost in a stupor. I was feeling I needed something else, I didn't know what, from him and he was getting ready to give it to me.

He reached down and put his hand on me and began to work his finger inside. "You are ready for me. This will hurt for an instant and then it will never hurt again." And true to his words, he began to push into me and as I began to feel myself stretch he suddenly plunged into me and I felt my body tear and burn and I began to sob.

"I'm sorry, Honey. It won't hurt anymore." He was very still for a few minutes and then began to move with a rhythm I wouldn't have believed. The pain and burning had stopped and I began to feel something wonderful happening to me.

"What is happening to me".

"Let it go, Honey. I'll be right with you all the way."

And then in a spasm of ecstasy, we both reached a pinnacle, held there for a few seconds, and then collapsed together.

Willie rolled over and pulled me up into his arms and caressed me as he talked. He talked about our being together for always and raising a family. I was having so many confusing thoughts, I barely listened to him. Here I am, 12 years old. A married woman and talking about children. I am just a kid myself. Is what we just did all that life is about? If I had a dream of something else, is it over for me? I never really thought about growing up. I was always so busy minding my siblings and taking care of Mama while she was pregnant, I never really thought about myself. Well, I guess I could just forget about myself. I now had a real responsibility that no one else could do. This will be my life from now on.

He wanted to love me again, but decided not to as he said I would be too sore tomorrow. So after a while, we both fell asleep.

Chapter Three

That was our nights and some of our days for the next few weeks. Willie went to work every day. I became a housewife and really had an easier life than ever before. We would make love every night and some times in the morning before he left for work. Willie was good to me. We lived like the other miners did - on credit with the company store from one pay day to the next. Never really had any money, but I was beginning to know some happiness. I was able to go to the store and buy things I had only imagined having before. I bought material to make dresses and undergarments. I purchased hose and shoes. I had always lived with a pair of hand me down shoes before. I began to look good.

I began to think this isn't so bad. I didn't have to work hard like before and I always felt that Willie appreciated every thing I did for him. He would tell me often how much he loved me and how happy he was. I couldn't tell him the same as I was still struggling with my feelings of whether or not it was love I felt for him. But I did enjoy our love making.

We would be lazy on Saturday, getting up late and eating a late breakfast. Then he would take me out and we would spend the day. Sometimes we visited friends - his, because I had yet to make any - and he would hold my hand as we sometimes would just walk and stroll through the woods and look and talk about the things we saw. As I said, he was well read and knew a lot about birds, trees and flowers. He would show me the wild greens that were safe to eat and we would pick them. I would cook them and felt so proud of myself. We were eating something I had never known of before.

Sunday was another grand day. Be lazy for a couple of hours in the morning, make love, eat breakfast and go to church. Because we didn't have a regular preacher, different members of the church would hold services in the small building we used for a school and church. Everyone was always happy to see us as we were the newest newly weds in the camp. Most of the time, we would go to Mama's for our big meal and visit with the family. Sometimes, we would go to Willie's mother's house. She was a widow and had a daughter still living at home. She always had a great meal but her home was sad. Not noisy and happy like mine had been.

This wonderful, happy time could not last. In no time at all, I found myself pregnant. When my menses stopped, I wasn't sure what had happened because no one talked about that sort of thing. When finally I mentioned it to Willie, he was beside himself. He explained to me we were going to have a baby. He was so happy. I didn't know if I was happy about the baby or not. I had just gotten accustomed to just living a new life with Willie. Things were changing faster than I could keep up.

John came by really often to check and see if I was OK. There was nothing he could do if I wasn't but at least he was showing his concern. Everything at home was just about the same except my next sister, Leila, was now taking care of the younger kids. Leila wasn't in good health so I was worried about her. We were always so close. John , Leila and me. Like three peas in a pod, Mama use to say.

Willie and I began to plan for our baby. I was sewing as much as I knew how. I would sew everything by hand and would try to make each and every stitch the same size. I was taught to sew but never took much interest until now. I was sewing for my baby. Willie would buy as much as he could afford at the company store. Sometimes he would bring home a length of cloth for me to make blankets and little clothes. Willie was so happy and so good to me, it was hard not to love him. And that's just what I did. I began to fall in love with my husband. At least I thought I was. I had no experience with a man before so I couldn't really be sure.

*   *   *   *   *

Life was not idyllic but it was what God had given me and it could have been worse. My husband loved me and I was pretty sure I loved him - if I had someway of knowing what love was about. I know he was happy and even though I missed my brothers and sisters, I was happy to be having a baby of my own.

Being pregnant was a new experience of course. I had gotten use to Mama being pregnant but I couldn't really see the change it made in her body. Now I could see how misshapen you become as the baby grew. I still wouldn't let Willie see me completely without clothes but he would pat my stomach and say I was beautiful. I had to laugh. Beautiful. I'm 4'11" tall and very much on the heavy side with child. My months of pregnancy were not too uncomfortable until my last one. My baby was due in January and by then I would be thirteen years old. I am glad I had the experience of taking care of my siblings. Otherwise, I would never have known how to start taking care of something so small.

My baby was not too large but I went down to the Valley of Death having her because of my short stature. I was in labor for fourteen hours but when the end came, I had a beautiful baby girl, with blue eyes and red hair. We decided to call her Mae. I had a sister by that name and I thought my baby looked a little like her.

Willie was not one of those miners who would go back out and gamble and drink with his friends after he had his supper. He would rush home from work and most nights stay at home to play and hold the baby. He was so happy that I had to laugh. I didn't know I could ever do something to bring such happiness to another person. I began to be proud of the fact Willie had wanted me and me so young. He must have really loved me from the beginning.

My days from then on were taken up with my baby and husband and I settled down for a life like my mothers. The cleaning, cooking, caring for the baby and Willie were all I lived for. Our nights of making love soon started up again and even though we wanted more children, we didn't want them right away. I didn't know anything about preventing pregnancy and Willie wouldn't practice prevention. But by God's grace, we didn't get pregnant again for almost two years. But I did get pregnant.

This time, I knew what to expect with the body growing and morning sickness which I had for a full three months. We still kept to the way we had lived before the baby came and I had gotten pregnant again. We slept late when we could, made love, and took walks and had talks. I listened still.

Now, I am taking care of my little girl, a house and a husband and being pregnant too. It wasn't hard on me though. In fact, it was easier than when I was with Mama. She had had her baby and there was really a house full there. Seven children. I think some of the younger girls were beginning to help Leila as she was unable to do all the work I had been doing. I was lucky with just my one. There, I had my brothers and sisters to care for in addition to keeping house. I still missed them but I was happy now.

Again Willie was so happy, he walked around grinning all the time. Most of our little camp would look at him and they would start grinning too because he was so happy. I was glad he was happy. He always made me feel that his happiness was because of me. He was such a good man and worked so hard, he deserved some happiness in this hard world.

When it came my time again, I had another long labor period and I had another girl but she looked more like me, dark hair but with blue eyes. We called her Edie. By now, I was fifteen years old.

I loved my girls so much I couldn't spend enough time with them. I would rush through the chores everyday and then would play with my children. I would put both of them on my lap and sing the old country songs that I had listened to all my life - Wayfaring Stranger, Barbara Allen, Lorena.

Willie would come in at night and see me sitting in the rocker, cradling my kids and singing. He would stoop by the chair and gather all three of us in his long arms with a big bear hug. How come I was so lucky to have such a wonderful, loving husband. But I soon found out God gives and God takes away. My happiness was not to continue.

Edie was only 3 months old, when Mr. Cooper came from the company store to tell me that my Willie had dropped dead in his store. Apparently, he had a heart attack. That's what they told me. But I later found out Willie had epilepsy. Epilepsy was a disease that no one knew much about so if a person had it, it was never talked about. There seemed to be some shame attached to the disease for some reason. And for sure, if it had been known, Willie would never have gotten a job in the mines. He probably had outgrown the attacks but I guess the ones he had in his younger years had weakened his heart. He was too young to leave his family alone like this.

Later I would ponder on Willie and began to realize why he seemed to be such a happy man and it took very little to make him happy. He probably knew he was living on borrowed time. But I had a stretch of living to do if I was to raise Willie's children.

Chapter Four

What in the world was I to do. Sixteen years old and two babies. The company would take the house from me because they owned it. Willie had no more than part of a week's pay coming to him. I was literally out in the street.

I just closed up the house and pulled down the shades and went into seclusion. I cried until I had no tears left. I would hold my babies and rock them and sob. Most of the time, all three of us was crying our heart out. They didn't know what had happened. They were crying because I was. Finally after a few days, I pulled myself together. I had to decide what to do to take care of my children. Willie had loved them so much, I wouldn't let him down by acting my age.

John came to get me and take me home. He was still at home with Mama and Daddy and he packed up what he could and we went back to live with them. They were overburdened as Mama had the baby she was pregnant with when I left, and she was expecting again in December. It was almost ironic. They had married me off because of the extra mouth to feed, and here I've come back, bringing two more. But what could they do? I had no place else to go.

When I moved in, I literally took over the household chores to help out. I had no income from the mines. And there was certainly no insurance. So we, the three of us, were the poor relations you often hear about. Mama and Daddy had thought they had placed me and I was out of their lives. Now, here I was back bringing my two children. Now they had three persons to take care of instead of one.

One of my biggest worries, was the charges we had made at the company store. I was still liable for that even though I had no money, no job and no husband. In addition to helping as much as I could with Mama and Papa, I began to take in wash. Some of the miners were unmarried and I could wash their clothes better and iron them nicer than a laundry so I had plenty of that. I began to slowly pay off the company store. It would be a long haul but I had to do it.

There were no institutions then to take care of the needy. When you fell on hard times, as we had, the family would take you in and mostly, you were treated very well. Sometimes you might start out with one family member and as time went by, you would be taken in by another one. That way the burden was not too great for too long a time. It's just the way things were done then. Most of the time, women remarried quickly. Especially, young ones like me. But I had no intention of marrying again. I had come to love my Willie and I would not marry another man that might mistreat my kids.

During this time, there was a lot of trouble in the mines and some of the men wanted unions and the owners were absolutely not going to sit still for that. They would close the mines first. The owners would send in "thugs" from up north to actually knock the miners back in line. There would be fights and "lock outs" so some of the men didn't get a full week of work. Everyone was scared and couldn't really determine what was going to happen.

We were only there a very short time, when there was a terrible explosion in the mines and Papa was killed. He was crushed and died instantly. We never knew if it was a planned accident or a natural disaster. Mama had just had a baby and his death was really hard on her and the smaller kids. And like my house, the mines took her home away from her. It didn't matter that Papa was a supervisor and had been killed on duty. That's why lots of the men wanted unions but it was too late for my family. So, she went to live with one of the older boys, who also worked in the mines, along with four kids.

Chapter Five

Of course, I had to leave as my brother couldn't take me in as well. I simply didn't know what to do. But we, John and I, decided I would leave my kids with Mama temporarily and he and I would rent this big house we knew about and start up a boarding house. There were always single men coming in to work the mines and had no place to stay so we felt it would be a good income for us. I was never afraid of work and although John couldn't do anything, he was there with me to prevent my reputation from being smirked. I felt this would be a good idea because it would give John some money also. He had lost his leg when a train ran over him as a boy and he wore a peg leg. He was a handsome man but so far he had not married because of not being able to make a living. I could also continue to do the laundry as I had before to pay off the bill at the company store and also do the laundry for the boarding house as well. I could see us doing very well here. If only I could take my kids in the boarding house but I wouldn't have time to care for them there.

So John and I went into business. I made beds, cooked food, packed lunches, cleaned and only was able to see my children once a week. I hated what I had to do but I couldn't see anyway out of it. I missed my little girls so much and the little time I was able to spend with them was not enough. I think my mother was kind to them but she had little time to spend with them and now, she was also a poor relation. Of course, when she went with her son, she had to take the rest of the children that were still at home. So the burden on this son was tremendous. Now she also had my two. But the money I was able to send her for the kids' care, really came in handy to help my brother take care of Mama. Occasionally, Mama would move to one of the other sons to lighten the burden on the first one. Of course, my kids had to go with her.

* * * * *

We didn't have any trouble filling up the boarding house. John had a small room and spent his time talking to the boarders. He would try to help me with whatever he could. It was hard on him because he would lose his balance when he tried to do anything heavy. I had a little larger room hoping some day soon to bring my kids in with me. The house had a good reputation as the men had a place to stay, good food to eat, as my cooking was improving every day, and had their clothes laundered.

Some of the men that came into the boarding house would try to make a play for me when they learned I was a widow but I would squelch that right away. I let them know that I was not part of the fee for the boarding house. I had kids I was trying to provide for and was not interested in men.

One man came in who began to show interest in me and I began to like him but I kept remembering my kids and I knew men didn't like to take care of other men's kids. I liked Charlie a lot. I was still just a young kid myself and sometimes I wanted to forget my responsibility and have a little fun. Some Saturday nights, Charlie and I would walk out together and we began to be known as a twosome but it couldn't last. I thought maybe if Charlie liked me enough, he would take my kids but he slowly pulled away from me since I wouldn't have sex with him without marriage. I still missed my Willie and I just couldn't push his memory away and trust another man by having sex and him leaving me. And then, too, what if I got pregnant again. No thanks. No sex. And sure enough, in a few months, Charlie did move on. He took up with another woman and left for another camp job.

I guess we had the boarding house about eighteen months, when an older man came to stay. He wasn't a regular miner but one of some consequence. He was a supervisor but he had no family. He had a wife who had died early in their marriage and no children. So he boarded with us. Then, he started to talk to me about life, work, children - anything and everything. He seemed like an affable man and I began to enjoy talking with him. He knew a lot about things in life as Willie had. He was tight with his money but he would bring me little gifts and trinkets. At the time, I guess I was too young to realize he was trying to seduce me. But then when he asked me marry him, I was repulsed by the thought of marrying this old man. But as the weeks went by, I had to give it some serious thought. This man could make life for my kids a whole lot better. He was old though. His hair was already white and he had a big bushy, white moustache. Mama was pressing me to come get my kids because they were too much for her to handle and she was only living on the gratis of my brother. I worried so about what to do, I prayed about it but nothing came to mind that I could possibly do. So, I decided I would marry this man for my kids.

Chapter Six

With a heavy heart and not really convinced I was doing the right thing, we sold the boarding house and John went into the nearest town. He got a little job with a general store. He could get around pretty good but at times had to sit and rest his leg. I was able to pay off my debt at the company store with what I realized from the sale. I got my kids, and David and I got married. We went to a really nice house. It was in the mining camp as all miners homes were but it was on the outskirts with the other supervisors' homes. It was the nicest home I had ever seen and we had some luxuries there. Nice furniture and floors but the toilet was still outside and no electricity. David said all he wanted was to make me happy and I didn't have to work hard any more. That was before the wedding.

Well, that first night was more terrible than anything I could imagine. My Willie had been so kind and good. This man was rough and took me with no time to ease my fears. He was like a bull. He said I had been married so I shouldn't mind whatever he wanted to do. But I did mind. I was a piece of his property to do as he wanted. He was so rough and through so quick, I never had any feelings at all like the ones I had with my Willie. I began to dread the nights.

What have I done. I thought we could have a good marriage as I had before. Or at least some form of kindness. I thought that my children would know this man as another father who would love and cherish all of us as we felt before. I was afraid I had made a terrible, terrible mistake.

Every night when we went to bed he would lock the door so the girls couldn't get in. He would keep me in there just as long as he possibly could keep up. Time after time, he would "make love" to me as he called it. But it wasn't love. Even in the morning, he was at me again. With my little children on the other side of the door crying for their mother. When he would finally open the door, the girls would wrap themselves around my legs and hold on to me. This made David mad and he would storm out in a temper.

My only salvation was my children. I kept remembering how wonderful a man Willie had been. This man I was now joined to was so mean. I don't know why he was that way. He had seemed so different before we were married. He said lots of things then that didn't happen. He supported us. He fed us. But he couldn't have loved us and been so mean to me in bed. Nor was he really kind to my girls. He was so short tempered with them. I wondered if it was because he was so old or because they were not his children.

My days were one after the other the same. I didn't have to work nearly has hard and David bought us nice clothes, but my nights were a horror. He wanted me waiting for him as soon as he had finished his supper. I was beginning to think it wasn't worth it but I had done this for my kids. I had to endure whatever he wanted. And he wanted it all. Now I knew what it meant when I heard "submit and endure". I was so afraid I would get pregnant. Since he had no children from his marriage, and I already had two, obviously David was sterile. But naïve as I was, I really didn't know what sterile was. I assumed I just didn't get pregnant. I prayed the Lord continued to bless me in that way. No children.

David never took us anywhere. When he came in, he was ready to eat his supper and go to bed. I had no friends and neither did my children. I could never have company nor have my kids playing with the neighbor 's kids. He didn't like for anyone else to be in the house. David was jealous if my family came around too often. He wanted me all to himself. Sometimes, he acted like the kids were in the way. I walked on pins and needles sometimes when he came in tired. I tried to always have the girls in bed before he came home.

I lived like this for about two years when I discovered that every time he could catch my oldest, Mae, alone, he would start to feel of her. Mae was only five years and didn't know enough to tell me. I decided I had enough.

I asked Mama if she would take the kids back again until I left town and found a job. Then I would come back to get them. She didn't want to. I don't know if she was afraid of David or not but she agreed to keep them for a little while. She couldn't understand why I was leaving a good man who worked so hard and took such good care of us. I told her the reason, but she didn't believe me. Women just didn't leave their husbands no matter what they did. But I just couldn't take a chance with my children.

So one day while David was working, I packed our belongings, taking the kids and their things to Mama and mine to the railroad station. I had planned on this for a few weeks so I managed to save some of the household money. I was able to leave a few dollars with Mama for the girls and I got aboard the train and just started riding. I finally arrived at a really small town that was cleaner than any I had ever seen. Obviously, the coal mines were out of the town or there were no mines so the buildings were cleaner.

Chapter Seven

I left the train and started walking to the center of the town and found a small restaurant. I went inside and asked for a job waiting tables or cooking or anything he had I could do. I had done it all at the boarding house so I was very confident I could handle any job he had available. The owner of the restaurant was an Italian and had newly arrived in America. He told me he could use me but I would also have to take care of his five year daughter. His wife had died on the way over from Italy. I didn't mind taking care of his daughter, because I really missed my kids and I thought maybe it would help time go by until I could go back to get them.

So here I am again, starting on a new life with the hope of getting my girls and providing a place for them. At this time, there were very few women who were not married at my age as by now I am seventeen years old. I didn't tell anyone I was married because I didn't want David to find me.

From letters I received from John, I heard that David was so mad when he found me gone that he actually went on a rampage all over the town to all the houses to see if I was hiding but he finally had quit looking for me. So when I began to feel safe, I would make the trip back to see my kids about once a month. I had to go and stay in my brother's house because I didn't trust that David had really quit looking for me. I didn't want to cause my brother and mother any problems but I didn't tell them where I was living because I was afraid they would be intimidated and tell him. Only John knew where I was in case of an emergency with my kids.

I didn't have much money and I couldn't ask for too much time off or I would lose my job. I tried to save as much as I could and would send some to Mama, through John, for my kids clothes and upkeep. Things were really rough on my brother with Mama, her kids, and his kids and mine as well.

I was gone about one year when I received a wire from John telling me to come home immediately. Mama was putting my kids in an orphanage. I dropped everything and grabbed what money I had saved and went to the train station. But when I got there, it was too late. John had taken the kids and rented a room until I got there but the authorities found him first. Mama had told them I had run out on them and had no husband to take care of them and they were put in an orphanage in another state. She didn't really know where they took them and they didn't want to tell me where they were. I had a really hard time finding out where my little girls were. I told Mama that I would never forgive her for what she had done. She pleaded that she had no choice since she was still with my brother and he was pressuring her to get rid of my kids.

I finally I found my children in Tennessee. I went to get them but they wouldn't release them to me. With no husband and no visible means of support, they were wards of the state. They did let me see them and all three of us cried our hearts out. They were clinging to each other and I to them. I promised them that I would come to get them as soon as I could, that I loved them and would not have put them there for anything. But the time came for me to leave and my heart was breaking.

It was such a pitiful experience, I never got over it. My two love children in an orphanage. How could this terrible thing happen to them. I tried not to cry, as tears have never helped me in any way, but I couldn't help it. As I walked away from the orphanage and watched my children watching me from a barred window, I truly thought my heart would actually crush. I had never felt such a feeling before and I was young enough yet not to know that heart aches would be plentiful for me in the coming years.

*　　*　　*　　*　　*

I went back to my job, which the Italian had held for me but I had to tell him my circumstances. He agreed because of my good work and his daughter liked me and because he felt sorry for me, he would let me have enough time off once a month to go see the girls, but that really cost money so I had to scrimp and save every penny.

I had no life of my own. I lived for my children. I was so angry with Mama that I didn't care if I ever saw her again. But then when I thought about it, in my heart I knew she had done all she could for me. She was actually at someone else's mercy in her circumstances. Her last child had been born shortly before Papa had been killed so she was in almost as bad a circumstances as I except one of her sons would always take care of her. Not to do so would be unheard of in a mining camp. But that doesn't mean he has to take care of his sister's children.

Chapter Eight

It wasn't long maybe a year when the Italian came to me to tell me that his brother had just been discharged from the army and would be staying upstairs in one of his rooms. The World War was over and he had come home. He had arrived in the United States unable to speak English but had "knocked" around enough with odd jobs to learn some of the English language to get by. Then joined the army during the war and had immediately become a citizen. So leaving the army, he arrived in town to be with his brother and he had gotten a position in the bakery and would be living there until he made other arrangements. The brother would have to sleep days as he was on the night shift and that his daughter, Maria, and I would have to be as quiet as we could during the day. We were use to singing and dancing when there were no customers to wait on and I guess we had gotten pretty noisy. Maria had to have a lot of attention, not having a mother and a busy father, so we would dance and sing to entertain her and keep her busy.

The brother, Joseph, had been there for a few weeks before I actually saw him. And when I did, I was soundly awed by this man. He was a typical Italian but so handsome. He had black curly hair, a black moustache and sparkling brown eyes. And he used those eyes to the best of his advantage. I don't think he missed anything in a room when he walked in.

Sometimes, Maria and I would forget ourselves and make too much noise and he would stomp on the floor or knock on it with a broom handle. When he did, I would make that much more noise just to irritate him. I was only a kid myself and I enjoyed playing with Maria. He thought he was so special anyway. I had seen the way the girls flocked to him and he responded to them. He was a real ladies' man.

I continued to go to see my girls when I could but I couldn't seem to get this Italian out of my mind. I tried not to look at him when he came in but he soon saw that I was intentionally avoiding him. He didn't like that. He liked for the ladies to look at him. One day, he asked me "Where do you go when you leave town? Do you have a lover?'

His accent was so thick, it was hard to understand him. But I had learned a few things in the way he talked because his brother spoke with the same accent and I could understand him pretty good. Also I had learned a little about men from watching them in the restaurant. Not much. But a little. And I knew he was trying to seduce me. Probably only because I was the only woman, so far, that didn't fall all over him.

"It's really none of your business. Go take care of your business and leave me alone."

But he continued to hang around the restaurant when he wasn't working or sleeping and it made it worse for me because I was beginning to be very attracted to him. I found myself making myself up some and being where he was at times. Then it got to be where he began to be jealous when any other male customer paid any attention to me. I was afraid I would lose my job if he didn't leave me alone so I stopped him in the hallway one day and told him. "If you don't stop what you're doing, your brother will fire me and I need my job. Please stay away from me."

"I can't," he said. " I see you in every loaf of bread I bake. I love you. I can't stay away from you."

"Well, I don't need your attention. I have enough other problems. I'm trying to get my------". I stopped. I had almost told him about my children. I didn't want him to know.

"What kind of problems? Maybe I can help. Tell me."

"NO!. Stay away from me."

I ran to my room and threw myself across the bed. I was miserable. I missed my girls. I was attracted to this man who I knew was no good for me. I had been told he had been married and probably was still married. I just didn't need this. God - help me. I don't want this life. I'm eighteen years old and I've lived a lifetime already.

I awoke the next morning with my clothes still on. I had cried myself to sleep and hadn't even gotten into bed. But again, I found that tear drops don't help. So I hurriedly washed myself, changed clothes and went to work. I felt awful all day and of course, Maria and her father could tell something was wrong. I tried to cover the way I was feeling, but it didn't work. Maria would constantly ask me what was wrong and her father kept giving me side looks.

Later that day, Joseph came to me and said his brother had told him where I went out of town. He apologized for asking if I had a lover and was so sweet that I couldn't be angry with him any longer. I just said "Well, now you know why I can't have anything to do with you."

"Why? Your life hasn't ended just because you have a couple of kids. You're doing all you can for them but you need a life beside them. You and I are an ideal couple. I've been married also but my life didn't end with the divorce."

"My kids come first. I can't think about myself. They didn't ask to be born. I have to get them out of that dreadful orphanage. "

"Well, we could spend some time together. Get to know each other ."

"I don't want to know you. I can't be hurt anymore." All the time in my mind, the thought was going around, I like you too much now.

"Believe me. I won't hurt you. Trust me."

Well, I did. He soon wore me down constantly hanging around me and in my way. We started spending time together when we were both off work and we enjoyed it so much. He took me to some of his Italian friends who lived in the town and even though I couldn't understand their conversations, they seemed to like me up to a point. I say to a point because all foreigners are leery of outsiders. And I was definitely an outsider. The Italians were a very close knit group.

He began trying to seduce me almost immediately and I held out for some time but I soon gave in to him. I knew it was wrong and my life could only get worse by doing this, but I just couldn't seem to resist him. So before I knew it, we were sleeping together. And as it turned out, he was only separated from his wife. I continued to work at the restaurant, he stayed at the bakery but we were together every waking moment. I had fallen hard for this man and he acted the same but could it be true? If so, why didn't he get a divorce? I guess she didn't want to let him go as he was a man's man. And a great lover. Or maybe he felt safe by not being free to marry again. He was certainly free with the wife he had. He did whatever he pleased.

And I. Well, I was also still married. I am sure David would serve me with divorce papers if he could find me.

Chapter Nine

As the weeks went by, Joseph started going to visit my children with me and we would go to see my family. We told them we were married and whether or not they believed me, I don't know. They probably didn't. But my family loved him dearly. He would send Mama cakes for her birthday and sometimes just because he wanted to for no reason. Probably he missed his mother. He had left Italy at 13 years of age so he probably began to think of her as being his mother. He really seemed to love them.

Anyway, I guess we got a little careless in our visits, as it was during these visits, David found me and sued for divorce with the reason being I was committing adultery. The papers said I was living with an Italian, claiming to be married to him when in truth, I was still married to him. Well, it was true. So without even going to court and telling what he had done to my little girl and the way he had abused me, we just let the divorce go through. But before it did, I became pregnant. I was only six months gone when I miscarried. I don't what made me lose the baby. I never had any problem with the other two unless

I was under so much stress that I didn't take the care of myself I had before. Anyway, I lost my little boy.

As soon as my divorce was final, and Joseph, in the meantime, also filed for divorce and it was completed, we were married. I was already pregnant again but I didn't know it. Also I didn't know that a friend of Joseph's living in this same town from Italy had sent to Italy to get her sister to come to America to marry Joseph. She was on her way here when all of this occurred so when she arrived, someone had to find a husband for her so she could stay. Anyone coming to America then had to have a sponsor or coming to get married and have a person waiting to marry them. Well, Joseph arranged for his friend to marry her. There were really no hard feelings. They all understood how things are done both in America and Italy.

As soon as our ceremony was performed, Joseph and I went to Tennessee to get my girls. There really was no problem. They just wanted to be sure they had a mother and father to take care of them. They were six and eight years old now. We were all so happy to be starting a new life as a family.

Chapter Ten

Joseph loved my girls and they loved him. They called him Papa as I had called mine. As time went by, most of the people in this town thought that Joseph was their father. He bought nice clothes for them and carried them around just as he would have his own girls.

The only problem we encountered was this little village of Italians, mostly from the same place in Italy. When we were married, I was treated rudely and scorned because I wasn't Italian. Seemed that all the couples in this village were Italian and Catholic and could only speak Italian. Joseph still spoke English with an accent but he would speak Italian to some of them who could not converse in English but he never wanted me or the kids to learn it. He had a real heavy accent but I loved it. I would wonder what they were saying to each other and maybe saying something about me.

We settled in a rented house and was able to furnish it a little. I had to quit work of course but Joseph was doing pretty good and we were getting along very well. I was so happy to have my children again. And as I said, I was expecting again. After the beginning three months of sickness, I was feeling very well.

When we made love, and it was often, it was the most astounding feeling. My Willie had been all that is kindness and gentle but even though he loved me most desperately, I didn't really love him as I had thought. Then, the marriage with David was a complete nightmare. But now, with this man - I loved him whole heartedly. I really knew what love was all about. When he held me in his arms, I felt all safe and such a wonderful feeling, I don't know how to explain it. I felt I had been running toward this time all my life because of the happiness this man gave me.

My first was a boy. Joey. Just about a year to the date of my miscarriage. Joseph was so proud. After he was big enough to go out, Joseph carried him around all over town to show him off. But he didn't take away his feelings he had for my girls. And they understood that Papa was proud of his son but also proud of his two girls as well.

I was able to dress in nice clothes and go back to visit my brothers and sisters at least once a year. I would go once and then they would come out once. At least I got to see them twice a year.

In a short two years, I was pregnant again. This time, another girl. We named her Maria after Joseph's mother. That is the Italian custom. The first boy named after the father and the first girl after the father's mother.

We had only been married a couple of years, when Joseph decided that he and I were going to Italy. He had never been back since he came over so he thought that to take me there would be a good trip and maybe I could learn something about the Italian people and his family could get to know me. The only people I had ever come in contact with were the coal miners and rail road men in my boarding house. He really wanted to see his mother. His father and older brother had come over a couple of times but he longed to see his mother.

We had planned for about 6 months and had made plans to leave the children and were almost ready when the most horrific of accidents could have happened did. My Edie was playing with matches when she caught her dress on fire and being the baby that she was, she didn't know what to do except run. By the time I caught her and put out the fire she was burned badly. We sat with her night and day keeping a mineral salve on the burns. Mostly her legs were burned where she bent over and tried to put out the fire. Months later, the doctor did a skin graft from under her arm and replaced the skin on her legs. It was actually years before she got over the burn but she would always walk with a limp.

So after this terrible accident, we never again planned to take a vacation. Having the children kept me busy at home and most of the time, completely out of money.

Chapter Eleven

But it didn't take me long to realize that this man I loved could never be true to me. He had been having his way with women for so long, that he refused to stop now. He would come home some nights when I knew he had been with someone but he would lie and continued to make love to me as well. But he loved our kids and I loved him, so I guess I couldn't expect perfection. I had never known it and probably never would.

The nights Joseph didn't come home, sometimes he stayed over at the bakery because work was good and he had extra bread to bake or he had another woman. How could I stand this? My Willie would never have done such a thing and I couldn't see how I was going to live in this situation. I spent a lot of time alone crying because he preferred someone else to me but even now, I didn't understand the way men were. It didn't matter if he loved me desperately, some men just had to have more women. That fit my Joseph. But Joseph had gotten my children for me. He was a good provider. So I guess I would just have to close my eyes. As much as it broke my heart, I would hold up my head, act as if everything was great and go be by myself and cry my heart out. I couldn't let my kids and my husband know how broken hearted and hurt I was. I even discovered that two of the children his Italian friend had were sired by him. That was before we were married but he still visited her at times.

*   *   *   *   *

Now it seemed that all four of my children were close but no doubt about it, Joey was boss. He had his way in all things. And I mean all. No matter what anyone else wanted, Joey won the day.

Well with at least one still in diapers, another girl, Louisa, came along. She was so different. Joey and Maria were the Italian looking ones. Now, Louisa looked not like me but like my sisters. She had great big brown eyes and reddish color hair. Her disposition was also different. She would let the others take over her life if they wanted to. She just wanted everyone to be happy.

We purchased a house, the one we were renting, before my second son, Jamie, was born and all seem to be happy. We were a loud family. Always with laughing, music, and of course, the Italian way, arguing. Joseph worked nights at the bakery and sometimes staying over at the bakery, I would fix his meals and one of the kids would carry it to him so he would have a hot meal. He would always send back something that he had baked there. We had six mouths to feed so we were always glad to receive anything he sent. The pay scale was not good and Joseph didn't make a lot of money, but a lot of people made nothing.

The Great Depression had begun and if you were lucky enough to have a job of any kind, you were indeed blessed. We tried to help other families because Joseph was always able to bring extras home from the bakery.

The husband and father of another Italian family had left them and they were hungry most of the time. I always had enough to send them something as well. I guess I felt guilty as it was her sister, Joseph was suppose to marry. They had been neighbors in Italy and we were neighbors here. She had a lot of kids and the sister who had come over and married another had moved to another state so she had no one to help. So I was glad we could help her. I had needed plenty of help as the years had gone by and I knew her feeling.

There were food lines in town and many families we knew were in the line. With the Grace of God, the job Joseph had kept us out of the food lines.

In those days, there were no government agencies other than the food lines to help people. People helped each other. But because money was always tight and we had so many mouths to feed including those of the neighbors who I took as my own, Joseph took a part time job on Saturday nights at a pool hall. He worked the food counter but also served food in the pool room where so much gambling was done. Saturday every man in town could be found in this establishment sometime during the night. Those nights, I would gather all the kids up and we would go to town on one of the back streets where so many families gathered. There were no places to go if you had no money so all the families gathered on one of the back streets in town in a well lit area for the women to chat and the kids would play. We talked about new recipes and what our kids were doing. That sort of gossip.

During these nights, I would send one of the kids to the pool room and ask Joseph to send us something to eat. He would always fix each of us a hot dog and soda. All of us, the kids and myself included, looked forward to this. It was the only time, we got restaurant food. Of course whatever he sent, came out of his pay.

It was on one of the Saturday nights I had gathered the kids together and gone down to chat with my neighbors that a call came that our house was on fire. I don't know what started it but we lost everything. I mean everything. The house was completely destroyed.

Lord, would I always have these terrible things happen in my life. Just when I made myself satisfied with my life, a new devastation came into it. What sin am I paying for?

Well I had to separate my family as our neighbors were taking us in. We were just fortunate that Joseph had some drinking and gambling friends and they rebuilt our house. But the house was becoming too small for our growing family anyway. We would have to make other arrangements soon. After Louisa, only two years, I had Jamie and then, six years later, my Annie was born.

Chapter Twelve

When I received the call, I knew I had to go regardless of the fact I was seven months pregnant and we had just purchased a larger house and was to move the next day. So, Edie came to supervise the kids and get us moved while I took my youngest daughter and went to West Virginia in the worst snow storm I could ever remember at the time.

I went by train and then had to take a taxi as the coal mining camps were usually nothing but a dirt path to the door. When I arrived, all the furniture had been removed from the parlor and there lay my Mama. I looked at her and knew that in spite of what she had done to my kids and to me, I still loved her. She had several strokes and had been in a wheel chair for seven years. So the last stroke had been her final one. But there she lay and had already met her Maker by the time I arrived. I had to forgive her.

My youngest sister was Edie's age and she was there with her son as were all the other brother and sisters. I tried to hold up as good as I could for my little daughter. I didn't want to upset her. She kept rubbing my face saying, "Please don't cry, Mommy". We laid Mama to rest and I visited Papa's grave for the last time. I knew I would never be in this place again.

When we returned home, the furnishings were moved and the kids were glad to see me. They said Edie had been too bossy.

*   *   *   *   *

This house was larger than any I had ever lived in (except for the boarding house) but was not nearly big enough for my growing family. We had two small rooms downstairs we took for the kitchen and dining room. Upstairs, we had four bedrooms and one bath. I now had five kids at home and another on the way. There was no heating system in the house - just small fire grates in every room. There was no hot water system. The water had to be heated on the kitchen stove for bathing, washing dishes and clothes. Each morning, I would get up before daylight, close all the rooms except the kitchen, build a fire in the kitchen stove with a few sticks of kindling and coal and get the kids up one at a time and let them stand in the kitchen by the stove to dress. Then urge them out so I could bring in the next one. Trying to keep them warm was a big problem and it seemed as if Annie, always had a cold or sore throat. We never went to doctors unless someone was bleeding. I treated the illnesses myself with what little I knew.

Well I am now 38 years old and having my last child. She's a beautiful little girl we named Jena. I am getting too old to have any more children. I think eight is enough. So I will have to do something about prevention. I didn't know what to do except abstinence. Joseph would not settle for that. He was now 50 years old but had not slowed down any. He was still having affairs and using me as well. But I could not possibly go through another pregnancy. I had been doing this for 26 years and didn't think I would last through another one.

Chapter Thirteen

It was late during the depression, when President Roosevelt started the CCC camps for boys all over the country to be able to work and make a little money that this small town began to boom. Boys came in from all over particularly Pennsylvania and the Carolinas. One that came from Pennsylvania snatched up my Mae right away and by some hand of fate, he was able to get a job at the post office so was able to get out of the camp. They had rented an apartment and were close by when she got pregnant and I was so glad they were. She had a hard time during her pregnancy and I was glad she was still with me.

It wasn't long after the baby was born that his mother wrote and told him that some factories had opened up in his home town so he took my Mae and the baby north to live. I was so upset and cried. Mae was 21 but she was still my baby. I always felt so close to her being the first one.

Edie was close to Mae too so she would go visit her when she could gather money enough. Edie was working at a clothing store and paid some board to me but she managed to clothe herself and go visit her sister who she dearly loved. She met a man in the north she really liked and I was afraid she was planning to stay north as well, but for some reason their feelings cooled down and she came home. Then, in a couple of years, she met a local man she wanted to marry. Papa told her he wasn't the marrying kind but she was able to marry him. He was some older than Edie but she wanted him. They moved into the downstairs of our house until their daughter was born.

*   *   *   *   *

The CCC camps were still there and these boys loved to party. Everyone could dance, some played instruments. My oldest son, Joey, could play a sax so he joined the band and played at the recreation hall on Saturday night and Sunday afternoon. And of course, we all got ready to go along and listen the music. Both of my girls, Maria and Louisa, were the best dancers in the town so the boys at the camp always had someone to dance with. Sometimes, if there happen to not be a dance on Saturday, we would move the furniture out of the parlor and held dances in our home, I guess that was about the happiest time of my life. I had all my kids around me but one, Joseph had a decent job and we were a happy, fun-loving family. We all loved music and parties.

The year was 1940, when my second youngest child, Annie, six years old, became very ill. There were only six kids at home as Edie and Mae had both married. We didn't know what was wrong with her but she was deathly sick. After about five days, the doctor decided she had an abscessed appendix. At this time, there were very few antibiotics. Penicillin had not been discovered as yet. The doctor completed the surgery but she had so much poison we feared for her life. She was in the hospital for four weeks, with tubes and needles in her arms and legs draining the poison. I was on my knees constantly praying for her recovery. Finally, she started to improve and we were all so happy to have her back home.

There was no such thing as hospitalization. However, the doctor was a gambling friend of Joseph's and was willing to do the surgery gratis. However, there was the hospital bill which we were striving to pay but I was undaunted. I had my little girl back

*   *   *   *   *

Mae's husband found an excellent job up north and they were doing very well. Mae was also working so she wrote and asked if the next daughter, Maria, who was only sixteen at the time, could come up during the summer and take care of her daughter while they worked. She promised to send her back home with clothes enough for her to finish school. So she agreed to go and I am so sorry she did or that we permitted her to.

Sometime during this three months, she was introduced to a friend of my son-in-law who was an older experienced man. He had been in the service but had gotten out and was now working. He was able to seduce her. I didn't know this had happened to her but when she wrote and told me she wanted to come home, I had to tell her we didn't have the money to send her. When Joey hitch hiked to visit with them, she cried and wanted to come back with him but he was hitching rides and couldn't bring her. She told no one what had happened to her so for the entire summer, she was at this man's mercy.

When Mae sent her home, sure enough she had lots of new clothes. But I knew when she came home, she had changed but I still didn't know the problem. Finally when she told me, I was heartbroken that I had permitted this to happen to her. That situation changed her life forever.

Chapter Fourteen

It seemed that bad luck or maybe just everyday problems seemed to assail us. One day when I was scrubbing the linoleum on our kitchen floor, my baby, just a toddler reached to the table where I had been using lye to scrub with and took the can and being the baby that she was, drank it. I didn't know what had happened until she screamed and I grabbed her and her mouth was burnt with blisters. We rushed her to the hospital and they pumped her stomach. Fortunately very little was swallowed but she was in misery. From that day on, she never had a well day. She would for no reason at all start to have nose bleeds. So bad some times, she coughed up clots. We had her to every doctor and none could tell us the problem. Of course, I clearly assumed something had happened to her during the lye episode but they could find no reason.

I spent so many nights praying for my baby and for all my children. They were my life and when she would start the bleeding, I thought she would bleed to death. Finally, when she was 17 years old, a doctor in another town found the problem. She had a spleen that was four times it's normal size and she had several small ones as well. After surgery, she never had another nose bleed.

Obviously, the lye didn't have anything to do with the nose bleeds. She had been born with the spleen problem. When we took her to the doctor, we always told him about the lye and I felt that maybe that distracted him from looking further into her problem.

Chapter Fifteen

1941 Pearl Harbor was bombed and World War II started and my Joey joined the navy. He had been working at the bakery with his father but just before he joined up, he got married. He married the sister of his friend. She was so young but so was he. He left real soon for training leaving his wife with us. She made her home with us and was another daughter with my two girls, Maria and Louisa. They were close in age. I didn't hear the two of them complain even though there were now three in a bed.

At this time there was so much going on. The world at war, all of our young men leaving, the CCC camp was closed because they were needed to fight the Japanese and Germans. You could hardly find any young men in the entire town. Anyone from eighteen to thirty-six was called up. We were given ration books and expected to use them for all necessities. My kids had one pair of shoes covered by the books. Sometimes, the younger ones could wear the older ones shoes if they were taken care of. No sugar, coffee nor gas. We didn't have a car so the gas didn't bother us. Sometimes, we could trade our gasoline stamp for one we needed with a neighbor who had automobiles.

So during this time when our world was upside down from the boys over there fighting and the rationing here at home, Maria decided to get married. In the very beginning of the war, she had been in love with a boy she met at the CCC camp. He was leaving for the army and they wanted to get married before he left, but we were able to talk her out of it. I've often wondered if she really wanted to marry him, if we could have talked her out of it. Or if she felt she had to marry because of what had happened to her. But I'm so glad we did because he wasn't overseas fighting very long when we found out he had been killed. She was devastated but managed to go on. I think now she felt guilty because she didn't marry him before he left.

She was never the same after her trip north and then the death of this young man. She was quiet and moody most of the time. Finally, she decided to quit school. I wanted her to finish but instead, she got a job and started working. Then she met another man, one that also was an older man. I guess she felt he would understand what had happened to her and he did. He had also been in the service but discharged due to injuries received during battle.

So now, I only had four of my children at home. All the men in the bakery were called up to the service but Joseph was too old to go. He had been in the first World War. So now he was supervising women workers in the plant. And of course being the man he was, he continued having affairs. I knew he had them many times before, but I always closed my eyes and didn't want to see it. I loved him so much.

Chapter Sixteen

When Joey came home after basic for a short leave, there was a round of parties. Drinking and dancing and playing music. We were having a grand time. Trying to hide our fear of when he returned. We knew he would be going overseas as the war was very bad. However, he managed to get his wife pregnant but he still left her with us.

I wrote to Joey every night. I knew it took a considerable amount of time for him to receive a letter so by writing every day, he was able to receive one every day. He wrote often but a lot of his had been censored and cut away most of the message. The worse part was not knowing where he was. We only knew that he was somewhere in the South Pacific. I also wrote to Mae every day. I still missed her but she was unable to come home for a visit. Edie and Maria both lived very close to me.

Right after Joey's daughter was born, his wife decided she would go to be with her mother. For some reason, she was upset about something and I didn't know if she was angry with me or my daughters. But then, I found that she had received a letter from Joey intended for a girl he had been seeing in California. I guess she had intended to leave him but I didn't know about all of this at the time. I thought she may have felt crowded as I didn't have a lot of room but we did the best we could. We treated her like one of us. My second youngest daughter loved her so much, she wouldn't stop crying when she left.

*   *   *   *   *

Except for the time when my children were in the orphanage, the next four years were the worse I have ever lived. I put the flag with the single star in my window to indicate this family had a member in the United States service fighting this war . Every day I lived in fear that the government would send someone to tell me my Joey was gone. The only contact we had were the letters he sent that had been censored so much you could not make out the meaning of the letter. I guess that was the intention. All the other kids wrote to him as well. We wanted him to know we loved and missed him so much.

Life was going on at home but not nearly as well. The other kids were in school living day to day, Joseph was working and still having affairs and he began to drink more and more. He had always like to drink but as he had gotten older, he couldn't hold it as well. So now, he was mean when he got drunk. Now I had to put up with his abuse. The little kids would get so scared when he started hitting me and screaming never ceased at the house now. I was about as miserable as I could be.

How can life be so cruel to one person. I had been married most of my life now and still wasn't cherished as a woman should be. I took care of my family. I loved them. But I suffered so much by my husband's infidelity. Maybe that's the way most men were. I didn't know. I didn't have the experience with men. But I do know that my earliest knowledge with a man, my Willie, was pure. He cherished and loved me. But God called him home and I had to go on. And how can you love someone, as I did Joseph, when he treated me so badly. Was there something wrong with me?

Chapter Seventeen

Well after about four years, Joey came home. He had changed. He didn't have a job and the places had promised to hold a job for the servicemen, didn't hold one for him. He had no skills as he went from high school directly to the bakery to the Navy. Now he had a family to support and no way to do it. He wasn't alone though. All of the boys coming home were unemployed. The jobs that the women had taken over during the war - they didn't want to give up. They got accustomed to having their own money and spending like they wanted. Not having to ask their husbands for money. And the companies didn't have to pay the women as much as the men and they loved that.

Joey had his mustering out pay and it seemed there was a party every night. Drinking and music. He didn't seem to be interested in saving until he found a job. Joseph loved this as it gave him more access to the women. And of course, Joey, like his father was like a magnet to the women.

Then when the money ran out, Joey took his wife and daughter and moved to Iowa where he heard about some work. He stayed a few months but nothing was there for him. Iowa is farm land. When they came back, his wife was pregnant again. He was receiving a little money from the government while he looked for work and in the meantime, his wife delivered another little girl.

Things finally began to look better for some families. The women were working. Some of the men were working. The government was arranging loans to buy homes, which they had never done before. The bungalows were being built and were all that a family could want.

Things had gotten worse for my family. Joseph had lost his job because they gave it to one of the veterans. He had kept the bakery running 24 hours a day for 4 years. Now he was too old to have a job. So now what were we to do. I was so worried over money. I still had two girls in school and no income at all. Joseph was now 60 years old and couldn't possibly get a job anywhere. The bakery was all he knew and that was the only one in town.

But some of the men, like my Joey, appied for government schooling. He decided he wanted to be a barber so the government would pay for his schooling plus give him a stipend to live on and the amount included whether or not he was married and had a family. Well that worked pretty good but the only place he could train for a barber was in the state capitol so I kept his children. His wife went with him even though she was so angry because of his infidelity. He was turning out just like his father.

After his schooling, Joey came home and opened a barber shop. But naturally, that didn't work either. I don't think he was lazy - he just couldn't seem to get going after the war. He didn't really know what he wanted to do. He talked us into going into the restaurant business as so many Italian families were doing but already he had started to become an alcoholic so he was drinking when he should have been working. He wanted to sell drinks in the restaurant and that folded that business. After that, he wanted to open a boarding house. That worked for a very short time. Then he was tired of that.

I was working very hard during this time as I still had two children in school and I would have to get up early enough to get them off to school and then go to the boarding house and start breakfast for the boarders. It was beginning to tell on me. But it wasn't long before that was a 'bust' as well. I was doing most of the work. I just didn't think we could get involved with any more of his schemes. We wanted to help but all we had was our home and I couldn't risk that.

It was during this time, that Annie, my 13 year old, met one of the boarders and they ran away together. We didn't want the police to know as it would ruin her reputation when she came back. They were gone from Friday through the week end when she came back. They had planned to get married but when they arrived at his brother's house, the brother told him to take her home before the police locked him up because she was a minor. True - she didn't look like a minor but she was.

I was beginning to think my child hated me. She would be so rebellious about anything and everything. I couldn't control her at all. My love didn't budge her.

So, after we closed the boarding house, Joey took his family and moved north where my oldest girl, Mae, lived. He was able to latch onto a pretty good job and was working another part time as well. After his move, we saw very little of him. Outside of coming home again where we had nothing to offer, he had to make it work.

After the boarding house episode, Joseph found a small job in the pool room. He worked there cleaning up and doing whatever was necessary to keep it going for a very minimal amount. I was able to get a job cooking in a restaurant. I worked the day shift so I could be home for my girls. But I was beginning to wear down. My body was not responding to the activity I was putting I through.

*   *   *   *   *

Now I was beginning to have problems with my second son, Jamie. He was not so much a womanizer, although he liked the women, as he was a gambler. He stayed out late, drank, gambled. But he was always kind to me. He was more on the shy side than his brother. So it wasn't long before he got in with the wrong crowd, got involved with a girl and got her pregnant.

He didn't know it until after the baby was born and she wouldn't let him see the baby unless he married her. He didn't have any question about whether or not the baby was his- but who knows? So he married the girl and that set his life down hill from then on.

During these days, I cried over my children so much I don't really know how I survived it. My husband was unfaithful and abusive when he drank, which was most of the time. My daughters and son was so far away and I missed them so much. Another daughter married a man wounded in the war and would never be able to work and support her. They had to move away so he could get into a veterans' hospital. My son was on a downhill crash with the girl he had married. Louisa had married a very good man but they had a child that was handicapped. Now my two youngest girls were coming along and the older of the two was beginning to act so rebellious. She was so much like her father.

She wanted to go to a party one Saturday night and I made the mistake of letting her go. She met a boy there that almost drove her crazy. She had already run off with one boy and I was anxious about her going out. She was only 15 years old and so wanted to be with him she would do anything. I never felt like she loved him nor he her. I think she just wanted to get away from me. But he joined the service and was scheduled to go away. She wanted to marry him. I convinced her and I don't know how I did it to let him go on, take his basic and she finish school. I promised if she would finish school, I would sign for her to marry him. Well, she did as I asked for once and when he came home after two years, she still wanted to marry him. So I had made the promise and I had to do it.

She married him and after he was settled with an apartment, she went to be with him. The day she left, Jena, and I cried a river of tears. I think Annie cried a little too. I think she knew she had made a terrible mistake and was just too stubborn to admit it.

Chapter Eighteen

All my kids were gone now except the one that had been so sick. She and I were so very close. I loved her so much but no more than the others. Joseph continued to drink. He had lost his job and was working in a pool hall for $4.00 a day. By my older one getting married, there were three of us living on that. Once, Annie arrived with her husband, she was able to get a job. She began to send me a few dollars every now and then and they always came in the "nick of time". We were really poor folks.

Louisa lived in a town about 50 miles away and because I was having so much trouble with Joseph drinking and my baby, Jena, was sickly, I decided to move to that town. Joseph didn't want to go but I made up my mind I was going. So we moved. I was able to find another doctor for Jena and he was the one who found he problem with her spleen. After all these years, a new doctor found her problem almost immediately. She had surgery and was a different person. In the new town, you could not buy alcohol so it slowed the drinking some.

So we had been living in the new location for about a year when Annie came home. She was ready for a divorce which I always expected would happen. Her marriage had been a terrible mistake. Once she was away from home, her husband abused her physically, drank and ran around with almost anything that would look at him. He had lots of women because he was a very handsome man but he was so vile and immoral. Annie had enough so she was home but she had not settled down any. She had no plans and work was at a premium in this town so I was able to convince her to go to Maria's to spend some time. Maria had moved away as her husband that had been wounded during the war had to go to the Veterans' hospital there. Fortunately, my Maria was such a good daughter and sister that Annie was agreeable. It didn't take her long to get settled there and find work so that she could start living again.

$$* \quad * \quad * \quad * \quad *$$

It was during this time that I received a call to come to West Virginia. There had been a terrible accident concerning one of my brothers' family. I had been feeling poorly for quite some time and it was such an effort for me to go. I guess it was about the second biggest snow fall I had ever seen (the first being when my mother died). Louisa, her husband, Edie and I piled into his car and drove the 300 miles in this terrible storm.

When we arrived, there were two coffins in the room with an aisle to walk down in between. My brother and his wife, who was pregnant, had been killed. Their youngest son was also injured but survived. My brother had twelve children and they were all there standing between their coffins. What a terrible sight! And I thought, I feel like I should be lying there too. My health was really deteriorating and I didn't know what was wrong.

I guess that was about the saddest thing I had ever seen.

We left soon because of the storm and it was only a matter of two months when my oldest brother passed. I kept thinking Lord why am I still here? I am so sick.

* * * * *

However, it was only a few months later that the answer to my question came. I had been having back aches for a long time. But because Jena had been so sick I never went to the doctor so when I was able to get to one, it was too late. But I didn't know it at the time. I had prayed many nights that if the Lord would just let me live until Jena was well, I would be ready to leave. So, the Lord had answered my prayers. I had been advised that I needed an exploratory operation, so Louisa called all the kids home. When I woke up, all my kids were there and I was told I would be going home in a day or two. I would be alright. They didn't find anything.

Well I went home in a day or two but I wasn't alright. I had terminal cancer of the liver. Annie came home to take care of me "until I was better" but I didn't get any better. I didn't know why and they kept encouraging me to eat and walk and I was constantly getting worse. Annie was there day and night telling me how sorry she had been so mean to me and was so good to me now. Joseph was so pitiful too. He would sit by my bed and tell me how much he loved me, knowing he had treated me so badly and was so sorry. Well, I soon began to realize I wasn't going to get any better. I knew I had to do some forgiving too. I told Annie and Jena, who were the only two around, to always be kind to their father. He came to this country as a mere child and really didn't know any better.

All the kids would come in to see me at different times, or call me but I never really felt like talking to them or being with them. I was in so much pain. Two of them were to give me injections for pain but the two older ones couldn't do it. Jena, the youngest, who had so many injections herself, was able to do it.

Well, I only lasted five weeks. The last night, when all were waiting for my last breath, I had gone into a stupor from the pain and high dosage of medicine I had to be given, but I aroused for an instant when I saw my brother, John, who had come to take me home. My favorite brother, who had always loved me without question and had died many years ago, was waiting for me. I didn't hesitate a minute. I loved my husband and children and really didn't want to leave them but I had so much heartache and pain, I willingly took John by the hand and let him lead me into glory to live for eternity. And you know, I always heard that there are no tears in Heaven. I found out for myself - it's true. No one cries here.

The End